In a Rush

Written by Catherine Baker
Illustrated by Neil Sutherland, Blue-Zoo and Tony Trimmer

H is running.
It is a long, long run!

She must get to the finish!

S spots H running along.
But H can not spot S!

S bangs into H.

An odd thing happens.
S and H link up!

D and **A** rush up as well.
d-**a**-**sh** , dash!

They dash off, but
D, **A** and **S** must stop!

H is still running.
She is hot and peckish.

C bangs into H.
They link up!

b-e-n-ch, bench!
Fab! H can stop and sit.

l-u-n-ch, lunch!
They get a big lunch. Yum!